MONKEYS
L♥VE TO EAT

FOR MY LITTLE MONKEY NIECES,
NAOMI AND JAIME

MONKEYS
L♥VE TO EAT

TREVOR LAI

[Imprint]
MAKE YOUR MARK
New York

Little monkeys love to eat!
But different monkeys like different things.
Take these monkeys, for example.

Milo loves crunchy food.
Mimi loves sweet food.
Max only wants to eat bananas.

Big brother Milo tries to set a good example.
He likes to eat a big bowl of granola every morning.
"Breakfast is the most important meal of the day!"

Mimi has a sweet tooth.
Just look at her pancakes!

And Max just likes . . .
BANANAS!

"MAX!!!"

Breakfast, lunch, or dinner, eating a meal
with the monkeys is never easy.

The monkeys love each other, even if they like different things. "Let's cook something together," suggests Mimi. "Then we'll all like eating it!" says Milo.

"Everyone loves BANANAS!"
yells Max.

Milo starts by making a fresh green salad.

Into a bowl, he puts lettuce, carrots, and lots of tomatoes.

"This salad is boring! Let's make it sweeter!"
Mimi drops in some strawberries and tops
it off with whipped cream.

"You can't put whipped cream on salad!"
cries Milo.
"Why not?" asks Mimi.

Now it's Max's turn.
What does he add to the salad?

"BANANAS!"

Milo tries making sandwiches.
He uses whole wheat bread,
lettuce, tomato slices, and ham.
Mimi looks at them and says, "Boring!"

She adds a scoop of ice cream and
a squirt of chocolate syrup.
Max adds a banana to each sandwich.

Nobody likes their lunch.

And everyone is hungry.

Milo has an idea.
"Let's make
a pizza!"

"We can each make slices of pizza the way we like it," says Milo.

"Cool!"
Max agrees.

The monkeys make a pizza together.
First, Milo adds broccoli, which is crunchy.
Then, Mimi adds pineapple, which is sweet.

Finally, Max adds bananas to his slices of the pizza.

CRUNCH! CRUNCH! CRUNCH! munches Milo.
"Sweet! Just the way I like it!" says Mimi.
Everyone loves their dinner.

The monkeys save room for dessert . . .

BANANAS!

Together, the monkeys make
the best banana splits ever!

THE END

THE END

IMPRINT

A part of Macmillan Publishing Group, LLC
120 Broadway, New York, NY 10271

ABOUT THIS BOOK

The art in this book was created digitally.
The text was set in Gill Sans, and the display type is Gill Sans Ultra Bold.
The book was edited by Erin Stein and designed by Jessica Chung.
The production was supervised by Raymond Ernesto Colón, and the production editor was Ilana Worrell.

Library of Congress Cataloging-in-Publication Data is available.

ISBN 978-1-250-08544-3 (hardcover)

Our books may be purchased in bulk for promotional, educational, or business use.
Please contact your local bookseller or the Macmillan Corporate and Premium Sales Department at
(800) 221-7945 ext. 5442 or by email at MacmillanSpecialMarkets@macmillan.com.

Imprint logo designed by Amanda Spielman

First edition, 2019

1 3 5 7 9 10 8 6 4 2

mackids.com

If you steal this book,
you will find the taste
of any food you eat
to be as bland as paste!